PALACE PUPPIES

Sunny and the Snowy Surprise

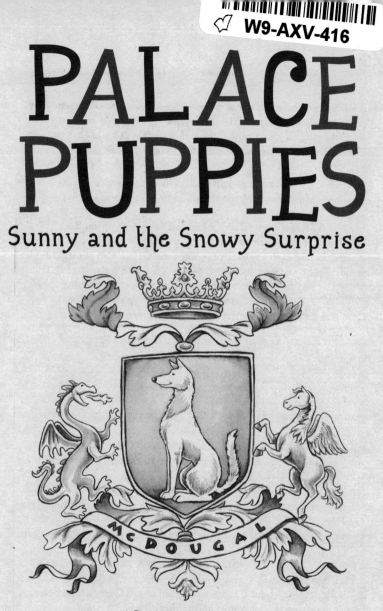

MCDOUGAL

By Laura Dower
Illustrated by John Steven Gurney

Disney • HYPERION BOOKS
NEW YORK

Printed in the United States of America
First Edition
10 9 8 7 6 5 4 3 2 1
J689-1817-1-13166

Library of Congress Cataloging-in-Publication Data

Dower, Laura.
Sunny and the snowy surprise / by Laura Dower ; illustrations by
John Steven Gurney.—First edition.
pages cm.—(Palace puppies ; 3)
Summary: On vacation at the winter palace, Princess Annie, Prince James,
and their dogs Sunny and Rex rescue three mischievous husky puppies, but
when the royals bring the huskies home, things start to get a little out of hand.
ISBN-13: 978-1-4231-6487-6
ISBN-10: 1-4231-6487-3
[1. Dogs—Fiction. 2. Animals—Infancy—Fiction. 3. Behavior—Fiction.
4. Princes—Fiction. 5. Princesses—Fiction.] I. Gurney, John Steven,
1962– illustrator. II. Title.
PZ7.D75458Sup 2013
[Fic]—dc23   2013012650

Visit www.disneyhyperionbooks.com

For Clark and Perry on Lois Lane,
Charlie on Rollingwood Drive,
and Torre, across the street

Chapter 1

"G roowwwf!" Rex barked at me from the doorway to Princess Annie's bedroom.

He chased his tail all the way over to my doggy bed.

"Get up, Sunny!" Rex tugged at my blanket.

"Rex!" I grumbled, eyes still half closed. "What do you want?"

It usually takes a hundred-piece orchestra to wake me up in the morning. But not with Rex around. He wakes up and runs wild before the sun rises. Rex is a beagle who just can't sit still. This morning, he must have been awakened by the blustery winds outside. Now that I was awake, I could hear them, too.

Rex and I live together at McDougal Palace in the kingdom of Glimmer Rock. Kings and queens aren't as common these days as they used to be, but I'm happy and proud to say that I belong to a modern royal family. My owner is Princess Annie. Rex belongs to Prince James. The McDougals have been the royal family of Glimmer Rock for centuries. We have our own coat of arms and everything!

"Come on, Sunny!" Rex pleaded. "I've never seen anything like this! You have to come look! Now!"

Rex stepped back for a moment, tail wagging. I could see him panting.

"Rex!" I growled. "Please get away from my bed."

"DON'T YOU WANT TO SEE THE SNOW?" Rex howled.

"Snow?" I hopped up and leaned into my morning stretch, paws pressed forward as I arched my back and yawned. *That sounded interesting.* My tail wagged a less grouchy good morning.

Rex barked. "Come downstairs! I want to show you!"

I shook my body hard. Oh, what a sleep it had

been! I'd dreamed that I was stranded on a dog-bone-shaped desert island with an unending supply of Beefy Yums. Just thinking about them made me as hungry as a . . . well, as a puppy stranded on a desert island!

"Sunny!"

"I'm coming, Rex," I barked back. "I *have* seen snow before."

"You have never seen snow like this!" Rex growled as he led the way out of Annie's bedroom.

We both flew down the large center staircase, sniffing madly at the air. I had to see this special snow Rex was talking about.

The carpeting on the stairs smelled like sweet jasmine. And baby powder. And there was this bleach smell, too, that got stronger as I reached the bottom of the staircase.

Winter was tough on palace floors. The marble got scuffed by boots and spattered by mud. This time of year, the palace staff had more than usual to clean up.

Rex scooted around a bucket of soapy water and a mop that had been left smack in the middle of the entryway. The large, circular entryway to the palace had marble columns and oil paintings on every wall. There were even paintings of animals and flowers on the ceiling!

"See?" Rex indicated the enormous picture window a short distance away. "Look at all that snow!"

I stopped in my tracks.

Wow.

Rex was right. There was snow, snow, snow, everywhere!

I'd never seen or played in that much snow. It looked as if the palace chef had vanilla-frosted the entire property.

Yum!

We headed for the library. I smelled the fire in the oversize stone fireplace—one of eight in MacDougal Palace.

Annie and James were playing checkers on the Persian carpet. Neither had changed out of pajamas, and they both seemed very focused on their game.

"I'm going to beat you once and for all, fair and square!" Annie cried as she hopped her checker over three of James's with one hand and scooped the trio up with her other hand. She spotted me out of the corner of her eye.

"Sunny!"

I raced across the room, took a flying leap, and sailed right into Annie's lap. My tummy grumbled.

The princess giggled.

"Well, good morning!" Annie said. She stroked the very top of my goldendoodle head. "Did you have a good sleep, Sunny?"

I burrowed into Annie's side. She was warmer than my dog bed! The beautiful palace was filled with all the dog toys and treats any puppy could want, but was there really anything better than *this*? Besides breakfast, of course?

Being a royal palace puppy was the best not just because of the food and fancy toys, but because of the people in the palace. I loved Princess Annie more than any dog bone. Well, most of the time.

But that didn't stop my tummy from its rumbly-grumbling.

Rex waddled over near me, looking for James's attention. But James was too busy plotting his next move in the checkers game.

"If I jump here," James said, thinking aloud, "then I get your piece."

"And I'll just jump you three times," Annie said. "Face it, brother, you're not winning this game."

"Hold on, hold on," James said thoughtfully. "Give me a minute. I still have a move."

All at once, Rex barked, backed up, turned, and ran full speed at James. He soared through the air, aiming for James's lap.

Unfortunately, he crash-landed right on the checkerboard instead.

"Yowch! *Rex!*" James yelped when the board hit him in the arm as it flew up and Rex flew down. The black and red checkers scattered everywhere.

"James!" Annie cried. "Look at what you did!"

"Gee, I guess we'll never know who won," James said, clearing his throat.

Annie made a grumpy face. "*I* was winning! You did this on purpose!"

"No, I didn't!" James said.

"ROWF!" Rex barked. He pawed all over James's back and then climbed onto his shoulders.

James tried to grab Rex by the scruff of the neck, but he couldn't get a good grip on that frisky beagle. He fell sideways onto the rug.

That was *exactly* what Rex wanted! He jumped on top of James and nuzzled his face and neck. Then he started to lick. I thought James would yell again, but he started to laugh. They wrestled on the rug, knocking the checkers all over the place. Annie lifted me into her arms and walked out.

"How about a big, big breakfast, Sunny?"

Finally!

My nose began to twitch. Did I smell apples? Ah! That was the lotion that Annie rubbed on her hands all the time. Then I smelled something else....

Bacon!

Rex smelled it, too. He and James scampered off together toward the royal kitchen. They were just a few steps ahead of Annie and me.

But who was that standing at the enormous antique cast-iron stove? I didn't recognize him at first. Then I saw the familiar words embroidered in black on his hat: *Chef Dilly.*

Palace pups are good readers, after all.

A stack of pancakes sat on the countertop, waiting to be served. I loved pancakes! I spied a bowl of freshly cut melon and berries and an entire tray of breakfast meats: not just bacon, but sausage and ham, too. Everything was crispy and juicy, and I could hardly contain myself. And then I saw the platter of cinnamon buns dripping with white icing.

Ooooooh! Those rolls looked like *they* were covered in snow!

"Roooooooorroroo!" I howled, too excited to keep my mouth shut any longer.

Rex twirled. Chef Dilly swatted him away with a spatula.

"Tsk! Tsk! Get down! The king and queen are dining in the royal conservatory this morning, waiting for you!" Chef Dilly said, trying to shoo us away with another utensil. "Princess Annie and Prince James, would you please remove these dogs from the kitchen? There is now drool all over the floor!"

"Sorry!" Annie said.

She hoisted me under her arm. James grabbed Rex. The four of us left quickly, before Chef Dilly got any more red in the face.

On the way down the hall, we passed by another enormous palace window. It felt as if we were looking at a snow globe. No one had ever seen this much snow falling so fast.

"Good morning, children," King Jon said, greeting us as we entered the conservatory. He raised a glass of orange juice. "A toast to Chef Dilly! Thanks to him, we have plenty of breakfast to eat on this snowy day!"

"Yes, and I have big news!" Queen Katherine added. "We're heading up the mountain to the

Winter Palace for the weekend! Nanny Sarah and Nanny Fran are packing your clothes right now."

"Winter Palace?" James exclaimed. "We haven't been there in ages!"

Annie and James had visited the Winter Palace before, but Rex and I had never gone. Today would be a very important day!

Neither Rex nor I have lived anywhere except McDougal Palace, but the royal family doesn't live in just one place. They have different homes all over the world! I'd seen pictures of a big penthouse apartment in the city and a private island off the coast, too. A puppy could get into some crazy adventures on a desert island.

Right now, however, we were focused on icy and snowy adventures! The winter palace sounded supercool. And not just because of the season.

I was happy that the king had put Nanny Sarah in charge. She would come up to the Winter Palace to watch the children. Nanny Fran was coming to boss us dogs around. Even Chef Dilly was coming, to cook good, warm food!

"Mother?" Annie asked quizzically. "I thought the Winter Palace was closed for repairs."

"It was!" The queen smiled. "But this week,

all the repairs were completed. Your new rooms were painted and filled with new books and toys. And now we have all this snow to play in! Isn't it wonderful? We can ski on Glimmer Mountain. You children can sled, too!"

"I always wanted to do that, but last time we went, you said I was still too small," James pointed out.

"Now you are just the right size!" the queen said.

"Our Winter Palace butler, Edgar, says the lake near the palace is frozen solid. Who's ready to skate?" King Jon asked.

"Me! Me!" Annie squealed with delight.

Annie told me once that she loved to do tricks on the ice, like twirls and jumps. I'd never skated with her before. I couldn't wait for her to show me how to do it.

Both the princess and prince seemed ready to take on any winter sport. Why not us pups, too? I imagined Rex on royal skis, buzzing down the mountain next to James. I'd be there in my ice skates, or on a sled. Way up high on Glimmer Mountain there were many things for the princess, prince, and pups to see and discover together!

My heart thumped hard.

"Rex!" I growled.

He had a hunk of bacon in his mouth. When

he tried to chew it all up in one gulp, he nearly choked.

"Rex!" I yelled again.

"I couldn't help myself! That bacon was whispering, 'EAT ME!'" Rex said.

But that beagle didn't stop at just one sliver of talking bacon. Rex went back for more! The second time around, he grabbed a pancake in his teeth, too. His paws slipped, and he sent an entire breakfast platter crashing to the floor.

"REX!" James wailed. "Not the platter!"

The maid was called. She cleaned up the broken china and brought a new plate of pancakes into the conservatory right away.

I was certain Rex would be punished, but the queen and king didn't make a fuss. Everyone was too excited about the upcoming trip to the Winter Palace.

After Rex's pancake mess, grouchy Chef Dilly brought out puppies-only breakfast bowls for us. I dug right in to the bowl of homemade kibble. Chef Dilly had put a minipancake on top! I was going to bark for syrup, but Rex beat me to it.

After we finished eating, Rex and I went into one of the sitting rooms. We couldn't stop talking about the snow. Through the windows, we watched it falling faster and harder. The wind outside had really picked up.

"I can't wait to go out," I whispered to Rex.

"I want to run!" Rex said.

"Forget running! Let's ski!" I suggested. "I wonder what puppy skis look like."

"Smaller than people skis," Rex answered. "And we need four of them, with four paws. . . ."

"Does the snow feel more like clouds or ice cream?" I wondered out loud.

"When have you ever felt a cloud?" Rex cracked.

"Well, It's probably colder than the ice cream in the palace walk-in freezer," I said. I'd gotten stuck in that freezer once!

"So what if it's cold?" Rex said. "Isn't that why we have fur coats?"

I laughed. Yes, my fur would keep me warm. But would the little pads on the bottoms of my paws freeze if I went walking on ice?

Maybe Rex was right. So what? I was ready to risk the cold. I was ready for a weekend at the Winter Palace. I was ready for all that wonderful SNOW!

"Rowwowwowoorrrroooo!" Rex howled.

That bark, of course, meant Rex was ready, too. Or maybe he was just looking for more to eat!

Chapter 2

"**C**alm down, Sunny," Annie whispered in my ear.

She had shut me into a large crate.

Rex was in a crate of his own.

I whimpered. Why did we have to ride up Glimmer Mountain in *this*?

So this was a weekend of firsts: first trip to the Winter Palace, first official truck ride in a snowstorm, and first ride in a lousy crate! I was a royal puppy. I didn't belong in this, did I?

The king, the queen, Annie, and James went up in an all-terrain palace vehicle, which had tires with huge treads that gripped the snow and ice. This special car made the mountain climb easier for *them*. But we puppies got stuck in a different truck!

Halfway up Glimmer Mountain, our truck stopped for a moment. Its tires were skidding.

I peered through the bars of the crate. I wagged my tail. Was Annie going to come? Could she see me? *Annie! Annie! Open the door! I'm in here!* But she didn't appear.

All at once, our truck began to move again. And thanks to our crate, Rex and I rested on pillows and blankets and didn't slip and slide at all!

Rex's ears drooped. "I don't feel so good," he grumbled.

"That's because it's so bumpy," I grumbled back. "And you have too many stolen pancakes in your belly!"

"Don't forget the bacon!" Rex said.

Suddenly, the road leveled off. Our truck came to a screeching stop, and Rex and I fell toward the front of the crate.

Ka-thump.

Next thing I knew, there was a loud *beep-beep!* The truck we rode in drove onto a long, winding path that was plowed clean. At last! A smoother ride!

I could see more now as we passed tall evergreens

heavy with snow. The forest up here seemed to go on for miles. There were no cars behind us. We went through an enormous black gate and stopped at a guardhouse.

The guard was an old man in a uniform who saluted the truck—and us puppies—as we drove through. He looked a hundred years old.

"How does the guard live in such a teeny-tiny house?" Rex asked.

"Aw, Rex!" I cried. "The guard doesn't live there! He lives *here*."

I motioned to the enormous palace that was in front of us. The truck had stopped in the long driveway. This place was astonishing. It looked as big as McDougal Palace, with towers and flags blowing in the wind. But here, there were huge stone archways on either side of the roof, too. And it was covered in snow!

The truck driver opened the door, and there was Annie. Hooray! She took off one mitten and clicked open my crate.

"Come and play!" Annie cried. "It's beautiful out here, puppies! It's a real winter wonderland!"

Then she opened Rex's cage, too. Rex looked at me. I looked at him. Without another moment's hesitation, we leaped from the back of the truck onto the snowy road.

Annie was right. This place was *so* beautiful. But it was also *so* cold. I wished my fur coat were just a little bit heavier.

We started sniffing around, slowly at first.

Then Rex went wild.

He raced through drifts of snow at the side of the road like he was a puppy plow! Snow flew every which way.

"Rex!" James called out, running after his puppy. "Slow down! Come back!"

I stuck my snout into the snow. It tickled!

Annie laughed. "You look like you have a beard, Sunny!" she teased. I felt the snow and little icicles clinging to my chin. The wind picked up loose snow and blew it around us in circles. After only a few moments, I was already getting used to the cold.

Up ahead, the Winter Palace stood before us with its columns and stone architecture. Close up, it wasn't quite as big as the other palace, where the royal family lived. But it sure was bigger than I was! I trotted toward it. The first-floor windows and front door were massive. What did it look like inside?

Sploooosh!

I fell to the ground, wet. Who just threw a snowball at me?

I turned to see Rex and James chuckling. Of course!

Thankfully, Annie had a snowball in her hands, too, meant for her brother. James could be such a troublemaker!

Swwwoosh!

Annie's snowball flew through the air and went splat on the ground.

Rex and James were quick to throw another snowball back.

Annie chased me behind a tall evergreen tree. I hid behind some large branches.

"THIS MEANS WAR!" Annie cried.

We worked together. I nudged wet snow with my nose, and Annie scooped it up and shaped it into a perfect snowball.

A few yards away, James and Rex did the same. And then we did it over again. We were hurling snowballs all over the place!

Annie got hit in the shoulder. I took one to the ear. Rex got one smack-dab on his tail! Ha! Snowballs whizzed all around.

The best direct hit was James. He got it right in the face! It must have been icy cold! He sneezed and rubbed his nose.

It was hard to keep up our stream of snowballs, but Annie and James kept rolling and throwing them.

Launch! Aim! Strike!

Snowball wars are fun. At least, until someone gets in the way. In our case, it was someone important. A snowball was launched from our side and James's and Rex's side at the exact same moment. BOTH hit the king!

"Oh, no!" Annie said, coming out from behind a tree. "I'm so sorry, Dad!"

King Jon's thick beard had snowy icicles in it, but he wasn't upset. He was smiling! The king's belly shook as he started to laugh. He bent down and scooped up some snow. He aimed for the stone steps of the castle.

"It's like being a kid all over again!" the king exclaimed. "When I was just a prince, I used to launch snowball attacks at the Winter Palace, too. But that was a long time ago." He picked up more snow and aimed for Queen Katherine next.

"Oh!" the queen cried, dodging. "That was long before we ever dreamed we'd rule this kingdom together!"

Annie and James raced toward them. A few more snowballs whizzed through the air, and I began to dance on my paws. They weren't cold at all. This was too much FUN.

Nanny Fran and a few of the other servants unloaded the trucks. They lugged in bags and boxes by the armful. I glanced up at the Winter Palace.

What was inside, waiting for us? I thought I saw something move in a window. Was there another palace puppy in there? I hoped so!

We followed Annie and James up the slippery stone steps. The big front door opened slowly with a creak.

Pine needles! Burning wood! Baking bread! There were dozens of wonderful smells hitting my nose all at once.

"Well, hello!" Nanny Fran said to the butler who opened the door. She introduced him to Annie and James. "This is Edgar," she said to us.

I guessed that they were friends. Many of the staff who worked for the royal family seemed to know one another, even though they worked in different royal homes.

Rex and I trotted into the dark entryway, and I looked around.

Inside, the Winter Palace felt different from McDougal Palace. Our regular palace was bright and gold, with shining banisters, and the ceiling was painted with bright scenes. This place felt old and dusty. Tapestries woven with pictures of unicorns and forests hung from the walls, and the curtains here were of heavy thick brown velvet. The sofas had wooden arms and legs in the shapes of lions and bears. On one wall in the Winter Palace there was a floor-to-ceiling mirror framed in gold!

When Rex and I went over to see it, he started barking at his reflection. What a silly dog! Did Rex think there was another beagle in there?

"Look at me!" I laughed, tossing my head to shake off the snow that was still on my fur. "I look like Santa!"

We heard Nanny Fran clap. "Rex! Sunny!" she called out. "There you are! Okay, puppies, I need to help Nanny Sarah unpack. You two are going to follow me. No wandering off! And no trouble!"

"ROWF!" we both barked obediently. But the last thing I felt like doing just then was put away clothes. There was so much snow to play in outside! I didn't want to stay in this dark place.

We followed Nanny Fran up a winding flight of stairs, however, as we were told.

"There are too many steps." Rex huffed and puffed.

I huffed and puffed, too. "I don't think we're meant to go pupstairs . . . I mean, *up*stairs," I said.

Rex laughed so hard that he nearly stumbled.

The stairwell was lit only by smallish brass lamps along the wall. It was a winding staircase, like a snake.

Thank goodness there was a bright white

light up on the next landing. Rex raced ahead of Nanny Fran to get there. We saw many rooms off the long hall. Bedrooms, I guessed.

Nanny told us we could explore a little bit. Exploring sounded good.

Large wooden tables lined the hallways. There were so many places to hide and snoop around in! We could have gotten lost in there if we weren't careful.

"Meeeeeeoooooooow!"

Rex and I nearly jumped out of our skins. A white cat appeared on the landing, its tail whipping back and forth.

"I'm Fitzsimmons, the Winter Palace cat," the cat said.

"Oh, hello," I said, trying to be friendly. "I'm Sunny, the goldendoodle. I belong to Annie."

"Hm," Fitzsimmons purred. He looked from me to Rex. "And who are *you*?"

"I'm Rex, the other dog. I'm a beagle."

"How lucky for you, *other* dog," Fitzsimmons said. "So, you both live in McDougal Palace, eh?"

Rex and I nodded. "We do."

Fitzsimmons told us that he had lived there at the Winter Palace since he was a kitten. He'd never been to McDougal Palace; he didn't want to go.

"No palace is as fine as mine," Fitzsimmons bragged.

"Hey, Fitz," Rex asked. "Did you see all the snow outside?"

"Yes, I saw it. But I hate snow. And I hate that hideous nickname even more than I hate snow," Fitzsimmons sniffed.

He told us he had a very important job: catching mice. His total mouse count was somewhere in the thousands! "I don't mean to brag," Fitzsimmons mewed, "but I'm the fastest cat in the kingdom."

All at once, he took off in the opposite direction. A few moments later, he returned with something in his mouth and dropped it on the floor.

"Ta-da!" Fitzsimmons announced, although his exclamation was a little garbled as he held the mouse delicately between his teeth.

Rex and I made a face. We wanted to offer congratulations. But what do you say to a cat when he's showing off his poor, dead mouse? Yuck.

"My stars! What is THAT?" Nanny Fran shrieked. She raced over and shooed Fitzsimmons away to the side. Then she scooped the mouse up and threw it into a trash can. "Bad kitty!"

Fitzsimmons weaved in and out, rubbing up

against Nanny Fran's ankles, and she instantly stopped being mad.

"Awwww," Nanny Fran said. "You're just being a helpful kitty, aren't you?"

I didn't know much about Fitzsimmons yet, but I knew he was acting like a big show-off. He sure knew how to get his way in this palace!

I'd have to keep an eye on that cat.

"Let's go outside again!" Rex pleaded. He tugged on my tail. "Let's find Annie and James and build a snow dog!"

A snow dog was just like a snowman, only shorter, with paws and icicle fur. Rex and I saw one in a storybook we had read.

"You can't go outside!" Fitzsimmons snarled. "In this weather?"

"But it's a snowy wonderland out there!" I exclaimed.

Fitzsimmons made a sour face. His whiskers twitched. "Be my guest, then," he said, purring again. "But watch out for snow *monsters*."

"MONSTERS?" Rex stopped in his tracks.

"Oh, there's no such thing as snow monsters," I said to Fitzsimmons.

"Tell that to the cat I know who was kidnapped

by the Ice Beast," Fitzsimmons said.

"Hmph!" I barked. "You're joking!"

"All I know is that the last palace puppy who visited the Winter Palace went out in a snowstorm and never came back." Fitzsimmons blinked at us, hard.

"Never?" Rex asked.

"Never *ever*," Fitzsimmons said, and he flicked his tail and scooted back out through the door.

"Sunny! Rex! Where are you two?"

Rex's and my ears pricked up. Annie was calling us from downstairs.

"Up here," Nanny Fran called back to my princess. "Just putting things in order!" Then she turned to us and softly whispered, "And getting rid of pesky cats and their mice, apparently!" She smiled as she reached down and petted us both.

"The mouse is our little secret," she said. "Now, you two go downstairs and find Annie and James."

So, we carefully scooted down the snaking staircase again.

The king and queen were on the couch in the front sitting room, enjoying the roaring fire. Edgar, the Winter Palace butler, stood there, too, with a tray of drinks. There was coffee for the grown-ups and cocoa with minimarshmallows for the kids. He had a bowl of warm milk for that cat, too!

But what about us? There didn't seem to be anything there just for puppies.

"Edgar," Annie said, "the puppies need a water bowl, too."

"The puppy bowls are in the kitchen," he said gruffly, "where puppies belong. I don't want a mess in the parlor, Miss Annie."

"That's not fair, is it?" Annie complained. "Why does the cat get to stay?"

"Fitzsimmons is the palace cat," the queen said. "Let's not cause a fuss. The puppies, as we all know, can get into a bit of a mess."

Grrrrrrr. I wanted to bark, *I'm not messy!* But I shut my mouth.

"Your Majesty," Edgar said to the queen, "if there's a problem with the puppies, we have a crate in the cellar. . . ."

A crate? In the cellar?

I gulped.

Rex was tugging at a thread on the carpet. I wasn't sure he'd been listening to any of this conversation.

"While we're at the Winter Palace, children," the queen went on, "we need to follow the rules. You need to listen to Edgar's rules."

"Oh, Mom," Annie piped up. "I know Rex can be wild. . . ."

"Hey!" James said.

"Yes," Annie went on. "But Sunny is one of the best-behaved royal pets I have ever met."

The king smiled and reached out toward me. He ran his fingertips over the top of my head. "I think Annie is right," he said to Edgar and the queen. "So we may have to bend the Winter Palace rules just a little bit this weekend."

Edgar cleared his throat. I could tell he didn't like what the king had said. "As you wish, King Jon," he said.

Annie kissed the king on the forehead. Then she leaned down and lifted me into her arms. I felt her fingers tickle me under the chin. I wanted to snap at her playfully. But I didn't. I wouldn't give Edgar any reason to think I was a wild dog!

I licked Annie's nose instead.

Rex jumped onto James's lap and nearly knocked the cup of cocoa out of his hand. Thankfully, no cocoa or marshmallows spilled onto the carpet! That would have been just the excuse Edgar needed to put us into the crate in the cellar.

Through the window, I saw the sun shine brightly on the trees and yard. The sky was as blue as an ocean. The snow had stopped, and the whole world glistened white.

"All right, children," the king said. "Why don't you take the puppies and go sledding?"

"What a good idea!" the queen agreed.

James and Annie gave each other high fives. It

sounded like a good—no, a *great*—plan to them, too. They raced to put on snow pants and proper boots for a sledding adventure.

Nanny Fran dressed us, too. We both had special snowsuits for dogs. Mine was bright yellow, with SUNNY stitched on the side. Rex's suit was bright orange, with the McDougal family coat of arms on it.

Nanny Fran smiled at us dressed in our bright snowsuits and said, "I wish I had my camera!"

Fitzsimmons was watching from a little way off. "What kind of snowsuits are *those*?" he cracked.

"Very fancy, very royal suits," I shot back.

"Those outfits could scare away the snow monsters," Fitzsimmons meowed.

Rex started to growl, but Fitzsimmons quickly scampered away.

For barking out loud! That cat was getting on my nerves! What I wouldn't have given for the chance to throw a snowball at *his* head. . . .

Rex nudged me. "That cat needs a taste of his own medicine," he said.

Rex and I agreed on this!

"Glimmer Mountain, here we come!" I howled as we headed into the cold.

Chapter 3

"Wheeeeeeeee!" Annie glided over the snow in her red sled.

Heading down the mountainside, we flew past groves of pine trees and clearings with nothing but snowy paths to sled on! The air was colder than I'd felt all day, so I nestled close to Annie on the sled.

I kept thinking about what Fitzsimmons had said.

Were there really such things as snow monsters?

"Waaaaaaaaah!" James and Rex went by us. They hit a patch of ice on the path, and their green sled flew into the air at an angle.

They came down hard, and Rex tumbled off. "Rroowoowoowowow!" he howled.

Birds flew
out of a nearby
tree with a loud
chattering. Every sound
up here echoed: birds, voices,
and the *THA-THUMP* of sleds landing
on the snowy ground.

Annie and I flipped over, but landed in
soft snow. I hopped off the sled.

"Let's go, Sunny!" Annie called back to me.
"Let's go for another ride!"

I started to shiver a bit, but I climbed aboard
the red sled again. My nose was running a little
from all the cold air. I leaned forward and gave
Annie a lick. She called those "puppy kisses."

I loved seeing my princess so happy. We raced
back up the hill.

The red sled really started to fly as we started
our second ride. We lifted into the air a little!
My heart was beating like a bongo. Whew!

The sled twisted and turned in the air.

"Whooooooooo!" I howled. I flew off, into a snowdrift.

When Annie came to a stop, she jumped off and raced over to see if I was okay.

I popped my head out of the snow and panted. "Ruff! Ruff! RUFF!" I barked, to tell her I was just fine.

I was having the best time. This was way better than hanging out inside with a pesky palace cat. There was no such thing as snow monsters!

"Look!" James cried out. "Rex is going to try to sled by himself!"

Annie gasped a little. "James, there's a dip over there. I'm afraid that maybe Rex will go over the—"

Before she could even finish her sentence, Rex's sled took off flying. He'd been strapped in by James, but that didn't help much. That beagle was hanging on for dear life. James's sled slid straight down the path at first. But then, all at once, it veered to the left. Rex let out a major howl.

The sled flew off the path and over a row of bushes; then it dropped clear out of sight!

"Roowowwowowowoooo! Rex!" I raced in that direction as fast as my paws would take me. "Rex! Rex!" I barked again, looking for my friend. Annie and James were behind me. But as I went through a thicket of snow-covered bushes, I lost my balance—and the prince and princess disappeared from view.

My paws slid along an icy pathway down the mountain. I landed on my bottom. It was like sledding—without a sled. Wow, my bottom was cold! This path took me down, down, down fast. In an instant, I was far from our sledding spot, halfway into the woods, with snowdrifts all around me. And I just kept sliding.

Why couldn't I stop?

I bit at the air, as if that might slow me down. But there was nothing to grab on to with my teeth!

Ba-bump!

Without warning, I smacked into a rock that was in the middle of the path, and landed on my back.

Ouch.

My head was spinning. My tail hurt. Where was I?

I glanced around. The edge of Glimmer Mountain was right there, just a few yards away. I could see mounds of icy snow.

Then, in the midst of all that white, I spotted a flash of green.

Rex's sled!

"Rex!" I slowly got onto all four paws and started to run toward the sled. I felt woozy. "REX!" I barked.

Something brown was there next to the sled. A paw? Yes! And then another paw, too! Rex gave a muted *woof.*

"Are you okay?" I asked.

Rex looked like he couldn't stand up, but he nodded to me. "That was cool," Rex said.

"Wait! Are you hurt?" I asked him.

He shook his head. "Not hurt," he moaned. "Just cold. *Brrrrr!* Like an ice cube."

I'd been really worried, and my heart had been pumping so fast that I hadn't thought much about the cold until now. I felt like an ice cube, too, but this wasn't the time to be making jokes. That Rex!

"We need to get back to Annie and James," I said. "They'll never find us way down here."

"Down where?" Rex yelped.

"I don't know, but we have to get back to the Winter Palace," I said.

Rex hopped up. "No! I want to go sledding again!"

I laughed. *"Again?!"*

All at once we heard something like a hum.

"Snow monsters!" I squealed.

Rex wailed, too. "Snow monsters! Noooooooo!" Then he stopped. "Wait a minute. What's a snow monster again?"

The noise continued. But it sounded less like a monster and more like . . . crying.

The sound was coming from under the green sled.

"Is someone there?" I called. I grabbed the sled in my teeth and tugged it out of the way. There was a hole in the snow! We listened closely.

"Roooooooooooo!"

"Rooooo!"

"Roooooooo!"

"Roooooooooooo!"

"You're right! I heard something, too," Rex said.

"It sounds like a *puppy*!" I cried.

Rex started to dig at the snow. "There's a hidden cave!" he yelped.

Rex poked his head into the cave to have a look around. Then he popped back out again. "Sunny," Rex said. "You won't believe what I saw."

"A puppy?"

"*Three* puppies!"

Chapter 4

Three sets of clear blue eyes peered up at us through the icy darkness.

Poor pooches! They were trapped! And they were shaking. Those pups were probably snow-cone cold by now. I shivered just thinking about it.

"Roooooooooo!" the pups cried out again. They'd heard us tromping around on the snow outside the cave.

"We're going to save you!" I barked.

"Roooooooooo!" they called back again.

Rex tried to extend his paw down into the snow, but the puppies couldn't reach. We needed something for them to grab on to. Maybe there was a stick that would be long enough?

I raced around the entrance and searched for a long branch to extend down into the hole, which wasn't that deep. With a little push, we could get the stick down in. It might help us get those pups out.

If Annie and James had been there, they could have reached in and pulled the pups out!

I glanced up at the graying sky. The sun had slipped behind a massive cloud. Something told me that more snow, *lots* more snow, was on the way.

"SUNNY!"

Wait! Was that Annie's voice?

"REX!"

James! They were both looking for us!

Rex and I howled into the air. "Rowf! Rowf! Arrrrrf!"

I scampered away from the cave's opening and let out a series of loud barks, to let them know where we were.

Annie and James heard my calls. They probably spotted the green sled, too, just as I had. Annie and James treaded carefully as they made their way down the incline. Annie was dragging her red sled behind her.

"Sunny!" she called out. "You're safe!"

"Where is Rex?" James cried.

Rex woofed. He was standing over the opening of the cave with a stick poked into the hole. He wiggled it around.

"Roooooooooooo!"

The three pups whimpered, louder this time.

When Annie and James made it to the bottom of the slope, they ran to us.

"Sunny! I was so worried!" Annie cried. She grabbed me with one arm and pulled me close.

"Are you hurt? Oh, my goodness! You're frozen!"

Like a Popsicle, I thought.

"Rex!" James cried when he saw Rex with the stick. "What's the matter? What are you doing?" He grabbed his beagle's tail. "Get out of there, Rex! We have to get home before the sun goes down!"

But Rex didn't come out to greet his prince. He tugged forward instead—while James pulled backward.

"REX!" James cried sternly. "Cut that out, or else I'm—"

All at once, with a pop, Rex flew out of the hole. James and the stick flew, too, and they both landed in a snowy bush.

"Yowch!" James cried. "What are you doing? When we get back to the palace, Rex, I'm going to make sure you never—"

"Hold on!" Annie said. She looked toward the cave where Rex had just been.

There was a faint whimpering.

From inside the hole, something furry poked its head out. Then three pups scrambled out. Rex's stick had given them a ride out after all!

Rex was a hero—and those newly freed pups knew it.

"Waaaawaaaaroooo!"

The pups tackled Rex in the snow as James and Annie looked on in disbelief.

Then one of the pups came over. His light blue eyes were fixed on all of us.

"You're huskies!" Annie cried. "Where did *you* three come from?"

The three pups were shivering.

"We can't stay out in this snow a moment longer," Annie said. "James, we need to get these puppies warm now."

"Let's use the sleds," James said.

He and Annie quickly piled the huskies onto the green and red sleds. Annie had a long pink woolen scarf, and she wrapped it around two of the pups. James took off his own scarf and wrapped it around the third.

Of course, we didn't get a free ride. Rex and I had to help the princess and prince tug those sleds back up the hill.

The lost puppies whimpered again as we very slowly climbed up the incline. Many minutes passed, but we made it to the Winter Palace path. The huskies were huddled together, shaking. I thought I heard their teeth chattering.

Annie and James stopped to take a break from pulling, and I went right over to the puppies and nudged each of them with my cold, wet nose. One of the pups looked up at me again with those clear blue eyes.

"Don't worry," I barked. "You will be warmer soon."

"Thank you," the puppy said. "We were so scared."

A few moments later, we started dragging again. It was much easier on level ground. In no time, we were at the front steps of the Winter Palace.

Edgar ran out to greet us.

"What on earth—?" he gasped.

"We found these puppies in a cave on Glimmer Mountain," James explained.

"More puppies in the palace?" Edgar cried, looking absolutely horrified.

"We need blankets!" Annie added.

All at once, the queen appeared.

"My goodness, what have we here? Are those Juno's pups?" the queen cried.

Juno was a sled dog who worked outside the palace, in the fields. I'd heard the king and queen speak about her before, and about how brave a dog she was. She usually slept in the barn.

"There was a lost cave in the rocks up on Glimmer Mountain. Juno's pups must have fallen inside," James said. "But how did they get there?"

"And how long were they trapped there?" Annie added. "They were all huddled together for warmth. They were so scared!"

"Let's get them inside by the fire, quickly!" the queen said.

The queen, princess, and prince each scooped up a husky pup and rushed inside the Winter Palace.

Nanny Sarah and Nanny Fran arrived with a pile of warm, woolly blankets. Each frozen pup got wrapped in his or her own. The three were placed on the rug in front of the hearth.

The queen called to Chef Dilly to prepare a delicious snack for all the pups.

Rex and I lay by the fire, waiting for the huskies to defrost.

That was when *he* appeared again, purring.

"What's happened here?" Fitzsimmons asked. "Who are *they*?"

"We found these pups in a teeny cave on Glimmer Mountain," I explained.

"Hmmmm." Fitzsimmons licked his paw. "I

told you there was trouble out there in the snow. I told you, but you didn't listen."

"Well," I said, "it's a good thing I *didn't* listen. If we'd stayed indoors, we never would have saved those puppies' lives!"

Fitzsimmons flicked his tail back and forth. "Show-off," he purred.

"Grrrrrrrr," I growled quietly. *He* was the real show-off.

Annie and James brought Rex and me our treats in a silver dog dish. We each got a bone-shaped chewie. The huskies got their own bowls, and the entire Winter Palace staff took turns coming in to the sitting room to see the puppies moving around, chomping on their chewies. The queen had one of the maids snap some photographs for us all to remember the moment by.

"I know these pups," Fitzsimmons purred. He seemed irritated by all the attention the huskies were getting. "They don't belong indoors."

Of course, I ignored whatever Fitzsimmons said and kept my eyes trained on the dogs instead. It was fun to watch the three baby huskies warming up.

I loved the way their brown, black, and white

furry ears stuck up in the air as if the puppies were listening to something really important, and the way they wiggled around on the blankets.

As they thawed out, the pups got more and more alert and playful.

James and Rex wanted a five-way wrestling match, and the pups were happy to join in. The little huskies kept biting each other's snouts and chasing their tails around and around until they all collapsed on the rug.

"I wonder how the pups really fell into that snow cave," Rex said again, thinking out loud. "How did they get so far from the barn?"

"Maybe they just wandered out and got lost," I said. "It must have been confusing when so much white snow fell so fast and everything got covered up."

"Actually, that's only part of what happened out there," a small voice squeaked.

I turned. One of the huskies was talking! His eyes were droopy, but they still sparkled blue.

"The truth is that when our mama left the barn, we decided to chase a bird," the husky said to me.

"A bird?"

"Yeah, and when we chased the bird, we kept looking up into the trees and we didn't see the cave!"

"Rowf!" the other two pups barked in agreement.

"Oh!" I cried. "What are your names?"

"I'm Axel," the husky answered. "I'm the oldest pup. My siblings are Blix and Chase."

"Gee, Chase sure is a good name for a puppy that runs after things," I remarked.

Chase laughed. "Sure is!"

"Oh, dear!" a loud voice called out from behind us. Edgar stood across the room with his arms crossed and a worried look on his face. "When do we return these mutts to the barn?"

"Mutts?" Annie gasped and grabbed a puppy. "They are not mutts."

"And they're not ready to go back to the barn," James added.

Edgar frowned. "Well, they cannot stay in the palace for very long. There are rules about this sort of thing."

I noticed Fitzsimmons between Edgar's feet. He was giving me an "I told you so" look. I wanted to growl.

"These huskies belong to our family!" Annie

and James said. "They can stay in this palace as long as they want."

Edgar let out a harsh laugh. "Excuse me, but I make the rules around here," he said sternly.

Fitzsimmons purred. "Mark my words: those huskies won't last a day inside this palace. And neither will you, Sunny and Rex."

And with that, he swept out of the room.

I was ready to blow my top. Just who did that cat think he was? We were palace puppies! We belonged to the princess and prince! We could do whatever we wanted, too! He didn't have any more rights around this place than we did.

"Don't listen to him," I said to the huskies. "We'll look out for you." I wagged my tail.

Rex wagged his tail, too, so they'd understand we were there to protect them. All at once, Axel, Chase, and Blix grinned wide, happy, puppy grins. Their tails began to swish back and forth like ours! They understood completely!

At that very moment, I knew Rex and I had found three new puppy friends.

No matter what happened, no fat cat could get in our way.

Chapter 5

After a second snack of chewies and flaky dog biscuits, the huskies settled down for a long snooze. Their little bodies overlapped in a pile on the sofa that went up and down with each small breath.

Annie and James fell asleep in their chairs beside the puppies.

Rex and I were the ones who were left to stand guard. Well, *sit* guard. Rex spent most of the time chewing on all the leftover rawhide. That beagle was always eating something.

Out of the corner of my eye, I saw something fall outside the stained-glass window.

Was it snowing *again*?

Yes! Rex saw it, too. He hopped up onto his hind legs as if he were doing a circus trick. Then he began to speed around the room in circles.

"Rex, stop!" I cried. He was running too close to the sleeping huskies! He was going to wake them up!

And sure enough, Chase and Blix stirred. They rolled right off the sofa, dazed.

A very hyper Rex moved right in to help out. But instead, he nearly flattened Blix on the floor!

"ROWF!" Axel barked. He got up on all fours and stood over Blix like a protective papa.

"Don't do that," Axel growled.

But Rex thought Axel wanted to play! He darted backward with a playful growl of his own.

"Rex!" I barked. "Sit down!"

Instead, Rex ran. He headed around the couch. Blix, Axel, and Chase took off after him.

Zip, zip, zzzzzzzip!

Three huskies and one crazy beagle slipped and slid on the floor and nearly crashed headfirst into a sofa leg. I got dizzy just watching them go, go, GO!

"Stop!" I barked again.

"Grrrrrrrrrrooooof!" Rex barked back before skidding to a stop.

The puppies crashed into him.

"Your friend is funny." Axel giggled, looking at me.

"He always wants to play," I said, shaking my head. My ears twitched. "But he doesn't always know when—or how—to stop."

"We love to play, too!" Axel said. "We've never played in a palace before. This is different from the outdoors, that's for sure."

I glanced at the chairs. Had all our hubbub woken up Annie and James?

My princess stirred in her chair, but stayed asleep. And James could sleep through the loudest snores. So the puppy chase had *not* woken them up. Whew!

Moments later, the pups were still wrestling. We needed to get them quiet. Perhaps a friendly, *quiet* game of hide-and-seek? Maybe we could do a short and silent tour of the palace?

We just had to be quiet, so that Nanny Sarah and Nanny Fran wouldn't hear us.

"What are *you* doing?"

I jumped, surprised. Someone was behind me. Fitzsimmons!

"You scared me," I said. I felt my pulse racing.

"You're up to something. What are you plotting?" Fitzsimmons said. "A secret tour of the palace, perhaps?"

I arched my back. *Could Fitzsimmons read my mind?*

"Be very careful," the cat said slowly, switching his tail back and forth in the air. "I have my green eyes on you."

"Yeah, well, we have our blue eyes on *you*," Axel piped up. "It's one cat against five pups this weekend, Fitz."

"You belong in the barn, and you know it," Fitzsimmons said. "And do NOT call me Fitz!" He let out a cough, and I thought he was choking on his mean words. But a fur ball came out instead.

"Eeeeew," I said.

"You know the deal," Fitzsimmons went on, pushing the hair ball aside. "You belong with the horses and the hay. I belong with the king and the queen."

Just like that, he turned and left. I heard him pad into the hall.

"That cat!" I ruffed.

"Ignore him. Fitz is always poking his twitchy whiskers into everyone else's business. He thinks he's so much better because he gets warm milk to drink and a palace couch to sleep on. Well, one day, he'll wish he'd been nicer to us!" Axel said.

"Yeah!" Rex said. "I hope so."

"Don't be cruel," I said, interrupting. Of course, I was thinking those same things. But when he said them out loud, I felt guilty.

"Hey, Sunny, maybe with your and Rex's help we can show that kitty who's really boss around here," Axel said.

"Well, I don't want to break any of Edgar's rules," I said.

Axel explained to me how Fitzsimmons broke rules all the time. He poked his nose where he wasn't welcome whenever he ventured out to the barn. Once, he'd tried playing a trick on the huskies—and gotten himself stuck in some wire fence outside the palace. Another time, Fitz had nearly gotten crushed by a giant, angry cow.

"That's what happens when you don't *moooo*ve out of the way," I cracked.

Axel smiled. "That's funny. I'm so glad you

found us on Glimmer Mountain. Even working dogs need a vacation once in a while. This feels like a vacation."

"Vacation!" Rex howled with excitement. "Let's quit standing around. *Ruuuuun!*"

The three huskies liked the idea. They whipped around Rex and the rest of the room like a tornado. Then they moved into the hall, sliding on the tiled floor.

Rex yapped and led the way for a while. But Blix wanted to be in charge, too. Then Chase got distracted and began racing something. I don't know if it was a gnat or maybe a flying dust bunny, but the other pups focused on it so much that they crashed into a wall.

Blix thought their four-pup pile-up was so funny that he got right up and pretended to crash into the wall again. And then he crashed into the gold-embroidered settee in the hallway that no one was supposed to touch. There was a sign right there in black and green: NO TOUCHING. NO SITTING.

Not only did Blix crash into it . . . he jumped *on top* of it!

I watched him prance across the seat, bouncing

up and down and sideways like he was doing a dance. The other huskies and Rex cheered him on. Then his paw got snagged on a thread, and the whole thing began to unravel!

Rex jumped up to help. But he didn't exactly succeed in helping. He started dancing, too.

"REX!" I barked. I was sure Annie and James would wake up now. Or perhaps Edgar or Nanny Fran would appear? Maybe even Chef Dilly would come running out, waving a rolling pin and shouting, "Stop that this instant, you bad, bad dogs!"

But no one came. I collapsed onto the floor. It was too exhausting chasing after

NO TOUCHING
NO SITTING

the new puppies and Rex. This morning had wiped me out.

"What's the matter with you?" Rex asked, standing over me.

I looked up at him. "You have to quit acting like a wild pup! If you keep this up we'll be sent back to McDougal Palace. We'll never get to ski or skate anymore. Just imagine if the king and queen had come in here! You could get us—and the huskies—into some serious trouble."

"I'm sorry," Rex said. He hung his head. "You're right."

"We're sorry, too," the huskies said.

The damage to the settee wasn't terrible, as doggy disasters go. I was able to nudge the threads under one cushion and make it look seminormal again. I used my snout and my paw to smooth it over.

Just as I got things back in order, the husky puppies ran all the way to the other end of the long hall, tails rotating like propellers.

They were headed upstairs!

"No!" I cried out. But the puppy pack scrambled up the winding staircase. The legs of young huskies may be short, but they're strong. I followed as quickly as I could. Thankfully, goldendoodles have strong legs, too!

The huskies and Rex had only a three-minute jump on me. But in that time, they managed to turn the entire upstairs upside down!

The moment I stepped onto the second-floor landing, I saw something white, out of the corner of my eye. I quickly realized that it was paper towels I was seeing! One of the puppies had gotten a roll between his teeth and torn it to shreds within a matter of seconds.

There was a trail of white paper leading to James's room. I followed the trail with dread. I could hear puppies giggling and chewing.

King Jon and Queen Katherine had put some of Annie's and James's old toys on display. The toys were now spread out across the room!

Axel was stretched out on the floor, chewing

on a stuffed monkey. Well, an *unstuffed* monkey, actually. He'd chomped all the fluff out of it.

Across the room, Blix and Rex bounced on James's bed and poked with their paws at a model airplane suspended from the ceiling.

"What are you *doing*?" I cried.

"Having fun," Rex said. "Let's go, huskies!"

On Rex's command, the puppies raced into Annie's room. I watched as Chase and Blix popped one of Annie's suitcases open. Clothes went *everywhere.*

"Let's play dress-up!" Chase said.

"No-o-o-o-o!" I barked.

Axel pawed at one of Annie's dolls sitting on the windowsill. Then Chase came over and bit into the doll; its head went flying. Finally, Blix caught his tail in a basket on a shelf. It came down hard.

Crrrrrrash!

Annie's costume jewelry and her little princess tiaras scattered on the rug. Rex swatted at the sparkly stones.

"STO-O-O-O-OP!" I cried again, louder this time. Then I rolled over onto my back with my paws up in the air.

"What are you doing?" Blix asked me. The other pups came and stood over me as well.

"I'm playing dead," I barked sadly. "I might as well *be* dead. This is a disaster."

Axel grinned. "Sunny, don't look so glum," he said. "We made the mess, but we'll pick it up!"

I flipped over. "How can five *puppies* tackle this mess?" I asked.

"Aw, this is nothing. You should see the barn sometimes!" Axel said. "Hey, Blix! Chase! We need to put everything back now. Let's go!"

Rex sat down. Blix sat beside him.

"You have to help, too," I growled at Rex and Blix.

"Sunny's right! Come on!" Axel shouted. "When we work out in the barn for our mama, we lift and help sweep, and collect things for the other animals. We push sleds and carry things. We take care of each other. We love working together. It feels good to be a helper to my fellow animals— and my family."

Rex puffed out his chest. "But I'm a palace puppy. We don't work."

"I want to be a palace puppy!" Blix chimed in. "I don't want to work, either. I want to play!"

Axel frowned. "We have to work, Blix," he growled, "that's our job!"

Blix convinced Rex to help out.

Working together, the five of us were able to move stuff back into the right rooms. I couldn't believe it! I was all paws when it came to folding clothes, and the dolls' heads were too hard to push back on, but we got James's and Annie's rooms into order. I even spent time clearing the hallway, using my tail as a broom. Axel taught me that neat trick.

We had nearly finished cleaning up when we heard a creaking noise behind us. Someone was coming up the stairs. I imagined it was Nanny Fran, wagging her finger at us.

But it wasn't Nanny Fran.

"What are *you* doing?" Fitzsimmons mewed as he came up to the landing.

"The question is, what are *you* doing here?" I asked.

"I live here," Fitzsimmons said.

"Catch any mice lately?" I growled. I hated how that cat appeared at the worst possible times.

"Mice? I just caught one near the kitchen pantry. And the queen gave me a special treat for my service."

Axel snarled. "Sure she did."

"Where is everyone?" I asked.

"Coming for *you* soon enough," Fitzsimmons purred. "They'll see once and for all that you pups are nothing but trouble."

"Grrrroowwwwl!" Without thinking, I leaped forward, ready to pounce on that cat. Unfortunately, when I jumped, I missed Fitzsimmons completely. I bumped into a large bookcase whose shelves were filled from floor to ceiling with potted plants.

And my worst fear came true.

All the plants on the shelves were knocked off—and the hallway turned into a dirt road.

Chapter 6

Needless to say, the plant incident made a little bit of noise—and mess.

In two seconds flat, Annie, James, and the others raced upstairs to see what was the matter.

Princess Annie stood there with a shocked expression on her face.

James stood next to her, looking twice as surprised.

"Arf!" I barked, first meekly. I didn't know what else to say or do. A little farther down the hall, the huskies rolled around on the carpet with one of Annie's scarves that had been left out.

Fitzsimmons went up onto a chair, flicking his

tail with pleasure. That cat sure loved to watch me squirm.

Nanny Fran pushed her way to the front. "Where's the disaster?"

The huskies stopped rolling around and sat at attention in the middle of the hall. They looked up at Nanny Fran and Annie with those big blue eyes. I sat beside them. My eyes got wide, too.

"Oh, my stars!" Nanny Fran exclaimed, clapping the palm of her hand over her mouth.

"What happened?" James asked, laughing.

Nanny Fran said, "What happened here, puppies!?"

James kept right on laughing. "Rex, did you do this?"

"Oh, Rex!" Annie cried.

Everyone glared at Rex, the usual suspect.

I felt terrible, letting him take all the blame. I stepped forward and nudged Annie's foot. I would confess to my involvement in everything: the torn settee downstairs, the paper towels, the dirt all over the hall.

But before I could say a word, Rex stepped up and pushed *me* out of the way.

"ROOOWF!" he barked, coming to my rescue.

Wait a minute! Rex was coming to *my* rescue now? Wasn't he full of surprises!

"All right, let's go," Nanny Fran said, shaking her head in disappointment. "Puppies, princesses, and princes! Downstairs! PRONTO! We need to change a few things around the Winter Palace— starting now. Let me clean up this mess. . . ."

I started to shake like a leaf. I hated getting into trouble. And I wasn't used to *causing* the trouble.

Neither the huskies nor Rex seemed to care much about Nanny Fran's scolding. They just tromped back down the snaking staircase as if nothing had happened.

Or maybe they smelled what I smelled: FOOD!

Nanny Fran led us to the kitchen, where we greeted Chef Dilly, Edgar, and Nanny Sarah.

"I'm not sure about a treat for *these* palace pups!" Nanny Fran said. She explained what had happened upstairs.

Nanny Sarah looked at Annie and James with a frown. "Chef Dilly prepared a Winter Palace feast especially for the royal family *and* our puppy visitors," she said. "I do wish you two had been more careful watching over the pups! They were your responsibility."

Hearing Nanny Sarah blame the princess and prince made me feel worse than before.

Edgar the butler stood to one side with his arms tightly crossed. I knew what *he* was thinking.

He wanted those husky pups, Rex, and me out of the palace. The glint in his eye said: *Now I've gotcha.*

All at once, the queen and king entered the kitchen. Everyone scrambled to look busy.

"What's all the ruckus?" King Jon asked his children.

Annie spoke up. She told them about the disastrous mess. She apologized on behalf of all the puppies, not just me. James said he was sorry, too.

"Well, even when the puppies make a mess, they are still a part of our family," King Jon said. "Why don't we just eat our meal and give our

husky friends a second chance? They've had a rough enough day already."

Queen Katherine rolled her eyes and laughed. "You can't resist a cute puppy, can you, King Jon?"

He smiled. "Nope! I have a soft spot for my furry friends," he said.

Annie winked at me.

Across the kitchen I spotted Fitzsimmons, lurking. He'd heard everything. It was as if there were steam coming out of his ears. His wish to destroy us had been foiled!

Axel leaned in toward me. "You and your princess are the reason we're not getting sent away," he said.

"No." I blushed. "I could have stopped Rex. . . ."

"It was us, Sunny!" Axel insisted. "We're not well

behaved, like palace puppies. You did your best to calm us down, but we couldn't help getting overexcited. That's how outside dogs act. We run around in the mud and hay all day. We don't know how to sit on a settee. You did your best to keep order. The queen and king know that. Don't blame yourself."

Axel was really clever for a small puppy. Being a worker dog made him tough, but so smart. I liked that. I wanted to be tough, too, like him.

"I wish I could see the barn where you puppies live," I whispered to him.

"Oh, no!" Axel said. "Trouble!"

Rex, Chase, and Blix had begun to play again. They'd begun a game of tag, making a figure eight between the legs of the shortest chef. Their tails kept thwacking his legs. The chef, needless to say, was waving his arms and shouting.

"Stop! Stop!" the chef cried out. He nearly dropped his tray of vegetables.

Fitz was loving this. I saw him sitting there, still as a statue, with his eyes on all of us.

"Wait!" I barked at the huskies. Axel was running around trying to help. But it was just becoming more chaotic. Didn't they see that this was a bad idea, playing tag in a busy kitchen?

Puppy tag involves a lot of chasing and ducking and lunging and . . . danger.

"Annie! James!" Edgar cried, clapping his hands. "You must deal with these animals! Now! *Now!*"

Was there no stopping these three huskies and Rex?

One spin led to another spin, and then, *CRASH*! A container of utensils went rolling across the tiled kitchen floor.

"AAAAAAAAAAAAAAAGH!"

All at once, another chef went flying into the air. The pot he was holding—and all the sauce in it—flew up as well. Then he landed with a thud. The pot clanked. The sauce went *SPLAT* over everything.

"Oh, my!" Nanny Sarah said, flapping her arms. Nanny Fran started chasing us with a wooden spoon.

The puppies still thought this was a game.

"AAAAAAAAAAAAAAAGH!"

The pups skided into another chef, who was carrying a tray of little pastries. Whipped cream and cake flew everywhere! All three huskies started to lick up the cream. I couldn't believe it when Rex joined them.

Of course, I wanted to lick it up, too. . . .

"Rex! Stop!" James cried.

"Oh, my!" Queen Katherine and King Jon exclaimed in unison.

"Out of this kitchen! NOW!" Chef Dilly roared at all of us pups, including me.

So we raced to the dining room.

Two enormous tables had been set up near a long buffet spread. The one thing any palace puppy loves more than a bone is a buffet. A GIGANTIC, wonderful buffet, where scraps always fall to the floor! And Chase wasn't about to wait for someone to serve her something. She smelled all the goodies on top, then bit the corner of a tablecloth and tugged hard.

"Watch out!" Annie cried. She saw what was about to happen before it happened.

But it was way too late.

The food went flying—including a basketball-size roast beef, which launched into the air like a rocket.

"Flying food!" the puppies yelped.

I watched the beef as it dropped back down, then started to roll across the dining room carpet.

"Oh, no!" another one of the chefs cried. His

face froze, as white as the snow outside the Winter Palace.

The puppies all stopped short and stared at the big roast rolling across the floor.

Fitzsimmons laughed. He tried to get an even better look by climbing onto a chair near the buffet. But something happened. Something unexpected.

In his rush to see all the mess, Fitzsimmons moved too quickly. His paw slipped, and when he tried to grab the edge of the chair, he grabbed a place mat that was under a tureen of soup.

Everything happened at once—the cat toppled backward and the big old vat of chilled tomato soup fell on top of him.

Splat!

"Fitzsimmons!" the queen cried.

Annie raced over and lifted the pot off Fitz's head.

Fitzsimmons let out a shriek. "MEEEEE-OOOOOOOW!"

"What a mess!" Chef Dilly declared angrily.

"No more pets at the buffet!" Nanny Fran cried.

"You can say that again!" Edgar howled.

Annie and James tried to calm down all the grown-ups. Nanny Sarah even raced in with an enormous towel to dry off the tomato-soup-drenched cat.

Rex, the huskies, and I slunk out of the dining room and hid behind a sofa.

The roast beef had come to rest in the doorway between the kitchen and dining room. One of the chefs hurried out and stuck a pitchfork-size kitchen tool into it, then carried it back into the kitchen. Someone else mopped up all the soup that had missed the cat and left a puddle on the rug.

I felt a little sorry for Fitzsimmons. The tomato soup had instantly stained Fitz's fur. The cat was quickly washed and towel-dried, but he was pale pink from head to tail.

I covered my snout with one paw so I wouldn't laugh too much at Fitz's new color. The three huskies were not so polite. They burst into laughter.

Annie tried to shush us, but it was no use.

Rex snorted.

Edgar looked angrier than a hornet.

"ENOUGH IS ENOUGH!" the butler cried.

We five puppies shushed up and huddled together.

Fitz went over to Edgar.

"Edgar." James jumped in, trying to calm the

butler down. "I think there's been some kind of misunderstanding, because our puppies didn't mean to do all that—"

"Out of the Winter Palace!" the butler declared loudly. "There will be no puppies allowed in this royal kitchen or in these royal quarters ever again! Ever! All puppies are banished to the barn!"

Annie and James gasped.

My eyes opened wide. *"The barn?"*

What had happened to the royal treatment? Nervously, I glanced out through one of the dining room's many windows.

It was snowing again!

Did we really have to go outside? What was the barn like? Was it big or small? How many animals lived there? Was Axel's mama out there?

I stared at the falling snow, thinking about today's winter adventure. I thought about finding the puppies and messing up the palace. It had been a day of unexpected surprises—and chaos. So I made a wish on all those snowflakes.

If we have to be banished, please give us an adventure we will never forget, I wished. Then I chuckled to myself. How could this day possibly get any crazier?

Chapter 7

"Out you go!" the butler squawked at us, waving his arms all over the place.

"No! No! Not the barn!" Blix cried. "I like it in here so much better. I want to live in a palace for always!"

"Oh, Blix," Axel said, trying his best to calm his brother down. "The barn is where we belong. It's where we've always belonged. Fitzsimmons was right. We only make trouble when we try to be indoor pups."

"Don't say that!" I said, even though I knew it was probably true. I was so mad at Fitz for being right all along! It didn't seem fair. And why did he get to stay in the palace?

Rex and Blix wouldn't stop complaining about the barn. They didn't want to play in the hay.

Normally, I would have preferred staying indoors, too, especially on a day like today. But somehow, deep down, I felt a little twinge of excitement about the barn. I really wanted to meet some new animals and ride on farm equipment outside the palace. I wanted to learn new tricks. Maybe Axel could show me how to be an outdoor puppy like him?

"Oh, Sunny, how will you ever survive in an old barn?" Annie wept as she hugged me. I licked her tears away. Little did she know I was now looking forward to it.

"Your palace puppies will be just fine outdoors," Edgar assured Annie and James. He turned to the canines in the room. "And you dogs can get into all the trouble you want out there!"

Edgar led the pups to a door at the back of the house. A short cobblestoned path led to the barn.

Fitzsimmons stood near the door, grinning.

"Off you go!" Edgar said opening the door wide.

Chase and Axel took off. They were halfway down the path on their way to the barn when

Axel turned and called back to me, "You'll like it, Sunny! Come on!"

I ran after him into the yard.

Edgar gave Rex and Blix a nudge, so they followed us, reluctantly.

I turned to look back toward the cellar door and saw the butler glaring again. He had never wanted us there in the first place. He'd said that from the start.

Fitzsimmons was still grinning. "See you later, *dogs!*" he called out to me and the others. Then he turned and flicked his pink tail.

The wind whistled around my ears, and I quickly pranced toward the enormous barn door. I had to get that cat out of my head. I hoped there would be something soft for me to nestle into once I went inside. I knew Axel would make everything work out.

Hey, at least one *cat*astrophe had turned out all right: Fitz was still the color of tomato soup.

"Hurry up, Sunny!" Axel howled. "I have someone here I want you to meet!"

I romped ahead. "Coming!" I barked excitedly.

Chapter 8

The barn was drafty and filled with way too many smells. This was nothing like the Winter Palace fireside rooms. The dogs had kennels set up along one wall. They liked to sleep with some of the other palace animals so they didn't get lonely. Each kennel was a wire pen with a plaque on the top that showed the puppy's name.

Juno, the mama husky, was still out working.

I couldn't wait to meet her!

Rex sniffed around the floor, checking things out. I sniffed alongside him. I smelled mud, melted snow, feed, hay, and yes, animal poop.

Eeeeewww.

Not even Rex, the adventurous one, liked *that* smell.

"I think maybe I'm a spoiled Winter Palace pup," he whispered to me as we checked out our new space. "This is too much farm for one dog."

I laughed. "Yeah, it smells a lot. And it's dark here. But we have to give it a try."

Even though I was cold—very cold—at first, Axel promised things would get better. He brought over a woolly blanket. Then he found me a quiet corner with a bale of hay. I stretched out on layers of straw. This would warm me up for sure!

"I'm glad you're here," Axel said. "We never get visitors."

Rex and Blix lay down for a short nap. After we'd all rested a while, Axel invited us on a proper tour of the barn. He showed us different areas where animals lived or where jobs were done. Off to one side was a special chicken coop. There were feathers scattered all over.

Quite by surprise, I came face to face with a spiderweb. I walked right into it, and it felt sticky on my snout.

"Bug!" Rex cried, when he saw something crawling on my ear. I shook my head until the spider fell off.

"So how do you like our home?" Chase asked me. She rubbed her nose playfully against my side.

"I like it; thank you," I said. "Except for the spiderweb."

"And the spiders," said Rex.

"It's not as nice as being inside the palace, though," Blix commented.

"You haven't seen my bone collection!" Chase said.

I followed her across the barn to a very large wooden bin. Inside were different bones in all shapes and sizes. It was like a puppy treasure chest.

"Where do the bones come from?" I asked.

Chase thought for a moment. "I'm not totally sure. My mama brings them back sometimes after sled runs up and down the mountain."

"Sled runs?"

"You know! Our mama, Juno, is one of the most important dogs around. She helps run skiers and supplies up Glimmer Mountain and all over the kingdom of Glimmer Rock," Axel added.

I was impressed. There was so much these worker dogs could do.

"Take a bone! I love to share!" Chase said.

I leaned in, grabbed a long bone, and settled down on the dusty barn floor.

"No lying down!" Rex cried, racing over to

me from the opposite side of the barn. He was jumping around happily. Blix was right by his side, laughing and wiggling all over the place.

"I'm resting with my new bone," I said. "Aren't you tired, Rex? It's been a busy day."

"TIRED? Are you kidding? There's too much to do to be tired!" Rex said.

I chuckled. Rex was acting friskier than the huskies!

"Look!" Axel barked.

We all jumped. Up in the rafters, I saw wings flapping.

"It's an owl!" I cried. I'd only ever seen them in books from Annie's library. But this one was real. It was perched directly over my head. And it was huge!

Rex and Blix ran and hid behind a wooden barrel. Scaredy-dogs!

Axel explained that an old barn owl lived up there. It was a perfect place to nest, especially in the wintertime. He also reminded me that there was nothing for any of us to be scared about.

"Did you hear that, Rex?" I called out to him.

Rex and Blix bounded back into sight. "Okay,

what now?" Rex barked to Blix. "What do you want to do?"

Blix pouted. "I want to be inside the palace again! I miss the buffet. And the fireplace. And the toys."

"But we have plenty of toys here!" Axel cried. He dragged out some knotted rope and began a tug-of-war with me.

High above us, a cluster of other birds rustled their feathers, and I jumped. Axel laughed. "Not you, too!" he barked.

"It's just . . ." I stammered. It was all so new, puppy life outdoors.

Rex, Chase, and Blix bit the rope, too. After we had played for a while, we five fell into a funny heap and began to roll around on the barn floor.

"Hey!" Axel cried. "I have an idea. Close your eyes, Sunny."

"Close my eyes?" I asked.

"Yes. You, too, Rex!" Axel instructed.

"Close them! Close them!" Chase and Blix cried.

"I want to show you something else," Axel explained to me and Rex. "On the other side of the barn."

"Goody! Goody!" Chase cried. She could hardly contain her excitement. What did Axel want to show us?

"Close your eyes and take ahold of my tail," Axel explained. So Rex and I got in line and followed each other slowly. That was because we couldn't actually see where we were headed.

It was funny how when I shut my eyes I could hear better or when I covered my nose I could see more. When I took away one of my puppy senses, another sense took over. Just then, everything was dark, but I could still hear the birds rustling overhead. I heard our paws dragging along in the dirt, too, with the occasional scrape of claws on the worn-out wooden floor of the barn.

And I could smell the barn in all its glory: straw and mud and wet animal fur. Yecch!

All at once, we stopped. Well, Axel stopped, and we all stopped behind him.

"We're here," Axel said. "Just keep your eyes shut until I say to open them."

I felt something hot. Was it hot *breath?*

I heard bells jingle.

I smelled . . . What was *that* smell?

Manure.

In other words, horse poop.

Rex and I opened our eyes at the same time. Whoa! Standing there in front of us was a horse. And not just any horse, but a massive horse. Axel told us he was a Clydesdale. This horse's hooves had little white fur coats on them. His mane was a beautiful furry white tangle.

"I'd like to introduce you to Titus," Axel said.

Titus neighed, loudly.

"And that's Phoebe over there, in the other stall. These are the Winter Palace horses."

"Wow," I said, looking up into the enormous brown eyes of Titus. "I've never met an animal this big before."

"This is Sunny," Axel said, introducing me. Then he introduced Rex, too.

"I've never met a royal puppy before," Titus replied.

"Pleased to make your acquaintances," I said to Titus and Phoebe.

"The pleasure is all mine, little doggy," Titus said.

"And mine!" Phoebe whinnied from the other stall.

A loud squeal came from the opposite side of the barn. Axel was pulling a giant sleigh!

He had a strap of leather in his teeth and was tugging hard. The strap was attached to the body of the sled. The bit in Axel's teeth was part of a harness. Axel told us that he needed to wriggle into the straps, so Chase helped out.

"Sunny, this is what a real sled dog looks like!" Axel explained once he was all set.

The harness was a little too big for him, since it had been made for his mama. But he could still move it around. A long piece attached to the wagon was what had made the squeaking noise we'd heard!

"Gee, Axel. You look like a real worker in that," I said, impressed.

Axel was destined to be a great sled dog. "Someday I'm going to be the fastest ever!" he replied. "I'm going to be as famous as Balto the sled dog!"

"Balto?"

Chase and Blix howled. "Our hero!"

Axel explained that Balto was the famous sled dog who had helped save the day for children in Alaska almost one hundred years earlier. Stories about Balto were known to huskies all over the place. Axel and his family hoped to be just as brave and hardworking!

"*You* want to try out the harness?" Axel asked me.

"Oh . . ." I mumbled, "I don't think golden-doodles are meant to drag sleds, do you?"

Rex pawed at the harness. "I do! I do!"

"A husky's life is work," Axel reminded Rex. "Though a beagle can do good work, too."

"But I don't want to *work*. I want to play!" Rex said.

Axel smiled. "Chase, let's show our new friends how to hook a load of cargo onto the sled. We can take our guests for a ride around the barn!"

This was a good idea. We all wanted to go for a ride!

"Hey," I said to Blix, who was sitting close to me, "what is your favorite thing about being a working dog? What do you like best about the barn?"

Blix shot me a look, then ran away. I was confused.

"Blix?" I called after him, but he'd disappeared through some loose boards into another part of the barn. I turned to the other two huskies. "What's wrong with Blix?"

"Just ignore him," Chase said. "He always does this."

"Does what?" Rex asked.

"He always runs away when the sled comes out," Chase said.

I thought that that was a pretty funny thing for a sled dog to do. Axel gnawed at the edges of the leather harness straps. He was ready to go, and he knew exactly what to do. Axel had been paying good attention to his mom.

Chase wiped off the top of the sled with her tail so we could all climb aboard.

But where had Rex and Blix gone? I didn't want Rex to miss out on the fun.

Finally, the two puppies reappeared, with their snouts and fur covered in hay. They'd been rolling around in the stuff!

"Where were you?" I asked Rex. "What happened?"

"I went to get Blix. He's still upset about being back at the barn."

"Why?"

"He doesn't want to be a working dog,"

Rex said. "But he's embarrassed to admit it."

"I think Axel and Chase already know how he feels."

Rex rolled his eyes. "Yes, but his mama doesn't. She says it doesn't matter what Blix wants: the only thing Blix can be is a sled dog, so he'd better get used to it."

I glanced at Blix, who was helping Axel and Chase with the sled. He pulled on a cord and fell backward. Then he climbed on top of the sled and slipped. Axel barked at him.

"Don't say anything, okay?" Rex said. "I promised I would keep his secret."

"All aboard!" Axel announced. "It may be a little bit bumpy in here, but a ride through freshly fallen snow will be just perfect!"

I settled in next to Rex, Blix, and Chase for my very first husky-driven sled ride. Axel must have been very strong to be able to pull all of us puppies and the sled, too.

"Watch out for the palace puppies!" I howled as we left the barn.

Outside, the snow whipped around our ears and eyes. I stuck my tongue out to catch a snowflake.

Chapter 9

Rex put his front paws on my back and tilted his head. "Oooh! Clouds!" he yelled. I looked up. The clouds were puffy now, like cotton balls. A flock of birds passed. More snow was starting to fall.

"Rowwwwwooo!" I woofed. It felt so good to be back outside again in the fresh air. Flurries swirled around us.

"Wheeee!" Chase howled.

Axel grunted. He continued to pull us along a snowy path that went around the barn.

"That's the cow stall over there," Axel said, tugging us to the right. "And that shed over there is where they store the royal farming equipment."

Everywhere, snow had covered the roofs and gardens in blankets of white crystals. It made the place look like a movie set.

Axel picked up speed a little bit. He pulled us over a big bump in the road. He swung out to the side and then back into the center of the path, and then he stopped.

"What's the matter?" I asked.

Up ahead, a tall evergreen had fallen across the path.

Blix, Chase, Rex, and I hopped off the sled. With a lighter load, we instinctively realized, Axel could pull more quickly. He dragged the sled right next to the fallen tree.

Rex had already climbed on top of the trunk.

"Be careful!" I cried out. "Those pine needles can hurt if they poke you!"

But Rex ignored the warning, and Chase and Blix followed him right onto the tree.

"Silly pups!" Axel said. "They never listen."

"Never!" I laughed.

Just then, one of the palace workers appeared by the tree.

"Shoo!" he said to the three pups. Rex, Chase, and Blix quickly ran away.

Then the workman spotted Axel. He obviously knew him well. "Hello, Ax!" he said. "Shouldn't you be back in the barn?"

"Ruff!" Axel barked, as if to say, *Uh-huh!* The workman waved him on.

Axel tried to turn the sled back toward the barn, but we hit a rock hidden under the snow, and the sled went tumbling.

And I went tumbling with it!

"Oh, no!" Axel cried. He got out of his harness and came over to me. "Are you all right, Sunny? I am really sorry!"

"Ouch!" I yelped. I'd landed on snow—but directly underneath it was a layer of hard ice.

"This is why you pups need to stay in the barn!" said the workman. "There are downed branches and trees. The king and queen won't like having their royal dogs out and about like this, not one bit! Come along."

None of the husky pups said a word. We had to hurry back on foot.

I followed Axel. Rex followed Blix. But as we started to follow the workman back to the barn, Axel whispered to me.

"Let's make a run for it!" he said.

"A run for it?" I asked. "To where?"

Axel winked at Chase, who squealed, "To the pond!"

The five of us raced away at full speed. We deserted the sled and harness in the middle of the path. The workman threw up his hands as we ran away.

"Time to play! Hooray!" Rex shouted as he chased his new husky pals into a clearing that led to Glimmer Rock Pond. "We can skate together!"

Chase got to the frozen pond first. She took the lead on the ice, where her paws kept slipping and sliding.

"Come and skate! It's perfect!" Chase called back to us.

Rex and Blix stuck together on the sidelines. I noticed that Blix was a little more careful on the ice than his sister had been. He didn't seem to want to go too far.

Axel explained why. Blix had been in an accident a long time ago. Well, last year.

"When we were really wee pups," Axel said, "Blix was helping Mama to pull some supplies onto the ice for a royal fishing trip. They pulled baskets and tools and fishing rods."

"Right here?" I asked. "There are fish here?"

"Under the ice," Axel said. "When it melts in the spring, everything around the Winter Palace turns a wonderful muddy brown and bright green. And the fish start jumping!"

This was not an average pond, I noticed. It was quite large. There must have been hundreds of fish hidden under the surface. Oh, how I wished I could see them, orange and brown and red, swimming underneath the water. If I was cold up here, I could only imagine how cold those fish must have been down *there*.

"So what happened?" I asked.

"He fell in the icy water," Axel said, shaking his head.

"Fell in!" I cried. "Was he scared?"

"On our way out to where the fishermen had set up their holes in the ice, Blix decided to take a little detour. He went another way, that had not been checked. The ice began to crack. It wasn't safe! Blix got nervous and couldn't move. As the ice cracked all around him, he fell into the water. Luckily, he was able to hold on with his paws to the edge of the ice. The fishermen grabbed him quickly, before he'd been in the water very long."

"But was he scared?" I repeated.

"Very scared," Axel said. "He never got over it. Do you like to skate?" he then asked me, extending his paw.

I blushed a little. "I don't know how."

"I'll show you."

Axel pushed forward and glided. His tail wagged as he pushed himself around and around, one paw in front of the other. Axel could do anything!

"Now you try!" Axel encouraged me. "You can be an outdoor puppy like me!"

I pushed forward and fell—plop—onto my belly. It was so cold. I shook off the ice and tried again. After about ten tries, I was able to skate—a little.

Axel smiled at me. "You did a good job, Sunny!" he said.

I blushed again. "Thank you," I said.

"Let's play ice tag!" Chase cried. She convinced Rex and Blix to join in, too.

Axel and I laughed.

Being afraid to go fast on the ice made me terrible at ice tag, because going fast was the key to winning!

Axel was fearless on the ice. He twirled and

swirled and waved his paws around. This outdoor puppy was a real ice champ.

Eventually, the sun disappeared completely, and dusk fell. I didn't like being on a frozen pond as darkness arrived. We needed to head back to the barn to warm up and get some rest. We'd been running around all day long. Even the friskiest palace pups could get tired out.

It seemed like a very long walk back to the barn. When we finally returned, I saw that the barn door was open. We slipped inside. A lantern that hung from one of the beams lit up the barn. Titus and Phoebe said, "Good evening." So did a pair of mice and the old owl.

"Watch out for spiders," Rex reminded me.

What a mess Rex was! His fur was snowy and matted and muddy! He was partly covered in broken bits of straw and dark grass from the walk home. I'd never seen him look worse.

Of course, I didn't look any better. I was just as dirty and straw-covered as Rex.

We gathered together in a corner of the barn and used our body warmth to heat each other up. It felt nice to snuggle close like that. It felt great to have new puppy pals.

Being an outside dog was nothing like what I'd expected. It was better!

I could bend the rules here. I could skate! I could sled! I could make friends with a giant horse!

Coming to the Winter Palace had given me many surprises, but I was pleased to discover the best surprise of all. And it wasn't even inside the barn. The best surprise of all was inside of me, Sunny, the goldendoodle. The best surprise of all was finding out that I was made for big adventure.

Before I knew it, I must have dozed off.

I awoke later, when something wet and cold nudged my face. I reached up with one paw and swatted. I opened my eyes and blinked.

"Hello, there, puppy," a gentle voice said.

Then she licked the top of my head.

Chapter 10

"Wake up, sleepyhead," the soft voice said.

I looked up into dark brown eyes and a soft face covered in gray fur. This dog looked just like Axel, only much bigger and older.

"Who are *you*?" I mumbled, blinking.

"This is my mama, Juno," Axel said. He stood over to one side, smiling from ear to ear. "I told her all about you and Rex."

I heard Chase and Blix cheering. "Mama! Mama!" They ran around their mother, tails wagging so fast that their whole bodies shook!

"Hello, Sunny," Juno said. "I'm the mother of these pups. Welcome to our barn."

"I'M REX!" Rex barked his own name loudly. Rex didn't want to be left out.

"Well, hello to you, too, Rex!" Juno barked back, grinning. "I didn't forget you!"

I stood up from where I'd been sleeping and blinked a few more times, just to be sure I was really awake. Juno was *beautiful*. Her fur wasn't actually plain gray at all; it was a mixture of gray and white and black. She looked so soft.

I shook out my golden curls, and some straw and dirt went flying. But most of the muddy muck was still on my fur. I shivered. All that skating had tired me out a lot. How long had I been asleep on the barn floor?

I looked over and saw that the other pups were as muddy as I was. Rex's fur was a totally different color from what it usually was!

"Sunny and Rex are delightful names," Juno said. She winked at us. "And you are delightful puppies, aren't you?"

"I guess," I said quietly, smiling inside. The only one who had ever called me delightful before this was Princess Annie.

Rex was nodding. "Of course we're delightful!" he barked. "We're always delightful."

"Not *always*," I cracked.

Axel laughed.

"Rex is a good, strong, royal name!" Juno said, gently reassuring my brother. "So it means you are strong and royal, too."

Rex smiled and wagged his tail. "Sometimes my owner, Prince James, calls me Rex the Great!" he joked.

"Great!" Juno said. Then she positioned herself so that her pups could all nestle closer. "Come here, my babies," she said sweetly.

"We missed you, Mama," Axel said.

"Yes, we missed you so much!" Chase added. She pushed her nose into Juno's middle and shook her behind. Blix nuzzled his mother's neck. Axel curled up by her paws.

Rex wanted in on the action. He pushed his way in between the others, and all the puppies began to laugh.

Watching them play, I began to think about my own goldendoodle mama.

If only she were with me now, I thought.

Annie has told me the story a zillion times. When I was a baby pup, just born, my mama goldendoodle went away from McDougal Palace.

She went to be a royal show dog, traveling all over the world.

The puppies made playful snarling noises. "Grrrrrrrr," Chase said, taking a bite at the air.

"Roooowroo!" Blix barked.

"Careful, you two!" Juno said. "It tickles. . . . Stop!"

But those happy pups didn't stop. They kept poking and wriggling around their mama. Then Axel crept underneath his mother's belly. He wanted her attention.

"RUFF!"

A frightened Blix jumped back and whimpered. "Oh, Mama, he scared me."

"Tsk-tsk!" Juno said to Axel. She placed her paw on Blix's body and pushed him gently toward his brother. "Kiss and make up, boys."

Axel and Blix rubbed noses, and everything was okay again.

"Why don't you join us?" Juno asked me. Without another word, she wrapped her paw around me and pulled me close, like the other pups. I felt safe. I looked up into her eyes. She looked so tired. But that made sense! She had been away on a big sled run for the past several days.

"So, tell me all the things you did while I was gone," Juno said. "Did Princess Annie take you for a walk to the barn? Is that how you met my pups, Sunny?"

"Well, not exactly," I said.

Axel stood up. His tail was between his legs.

"We have something to tell you, Mama," Axel admitted. "When you went on the sled run, Chase, Blix, and I . . ."

Juno frowned. "I have a feeling I won't like this."

"We left the barn."

"Axel! Oh! I put you in charge! I told you three to stay put," Juno said. She tilted her head and squinted at the pups. "Tell me what happened."

Axel swayed from paw to paw. "Well, we were waiting here, like you said. And then Chase saw this bird. . . ."

"A bird?" Juno cried.

"A red bird! But it was so pretty, Mama," Axel explained.

"Pretty, pretty!" Blix said.

"And we followed it into the woods!" Chase added, bouncing up and down.

"The woods?!" Juno said.

"And then we walked and walked and ended up in the middle of nowhere," Axel went on. "We were looking up at the bird, but then we lost the way. It was only snowing a little bit when we left, but once we got out, there was a big, *big* storm. . . ."

"It was *sooooo* big!" Chase said.

"There was snow everywhere! We couldn't see!" Blix added.

"We couldn't hear!" Axel said. "We had to hide."

"I know that storm," Juno said. "It was windy on top of Glimmer Mountain. The skiers had to wait before coming down, and the campers called off a day trip to the top."

"Yeah, and, well, during the storm, we fell into a cave," Axel admitted.

Juno leaned back as if she were thinking extra hard; her eyes opened wide.

"Well, you pups had quite the adventure, didn't you?" Juno said. "I take it—since you are all standing here in the barn—that you made it out of the cave?"

"We sure did, Mama," Axel said.

The other two puppies huddled together and nodded.

"Actually, we saved them," Rex bragged.

Juno looked at Rex and smiled. "Oh? Tell me about it."

Rex began to talk. He danced in a circle. He stood up on his hind legs. He rolled on the floor. He didn't leave out a single detail. He did add a few that hadn't actually happened.

Axel, Blix, Chase, and I just sat there, listening and not speaking. The more Rex talked, the more he exaggerated. It was funny, so we let him roll.

"And then, I pulled each of the pups to safety, with my teeth!" Rex explained. "They were all crying, but I calmed them down by singing a song. I can sing, you know. . . ."

"Sing? Well!" Juno exclaimed.

I snickered. Rex shot me a hard look. "Quit laughing, Sunny," he warned. "I'm telling Juno what happened—not you."

All at once, the other three pups burst into laughter. They jumped on top of Rex. He wailed as they nipped at his ears.

"Settle down! Settle down!" Juno said. "I think I've heard enough, Rex. That was some story! But everything seems to have worked out in the end."

"And now you're back!" Axel said. "That's the best part."

Mama Juno looked us pups over. We were quite a sight.

"My goodness, you are very dirty puppies, aren't you?" Juno observed, picking at our fur a little. "I'm sure the king and queen won't be too happy about this."

We all huddled together while Juno tried to clean us up the best she could.

"I want to thank you, Rex, for saving my puppies," Juno whispered. "And Sunny, too."

"You're welcome," we told her, proudly holding our muddy heads up high.

For a brief moment, I thought, life here in the barn was better than life in the palace. I could have stayed here forever!

But that wasn't true. I couldn't stay here forever. Eventually, I'd miss the palace too much. I'd miss my comfy doggy bed back at McDougal Palace. I'd miss my royal meals and treats and the topiaries in the garden, cut in the shape of all my favorite dogs. I'd miss the endless supply of Beefy Yums.

Mostly, I'd miss Princess Annie and Prince James.

As much as I was enjoying our day with the huskies, there were too many things about the palace I was not ready to leave behind. Once a palace puppy, always a palace puppy.

I knew Rex felt the same. He was ready to return home, too. What I didn't know was that at that moment someone *else* was also ready to leave the barn and go back to the palace.

"Mama," Blix said, "would you be mad if I told you something?"

"What, dear?" Juno cooed. "I won't get mad if you tell me the truth."

Blix puffed out his husky-dog chest. His eyes got very wide. "I don't want to be Balto."

"What?" Juno said, cocking her head to one side.

"I don't want to live in a barn. I want to live in a palace."

"Oh, my," Juno said. She looked surprised. "You want to live in the Winter Palace?"

"Well, not exactly . . ." Blix admitted. "I want to go with Rex."

"You want to leave behind Titus and Phoebe and Fitzsimmons?"

"Leave Fitz? Uh . . . yes!"

Chase and Axel giggled.

"But you would also be leaving the barn and your family," Juno said.

"No!" Blix cried. "I don't really want to leave you, but . . ." He lowered his gaze to the barn floor. "Forget it, Mama. I won't go."

Juno went over to Blix and nudged him with her front paw.

"Oh, Blix," Juno said. "We have a wonderful life here. We're huskies, and we pull the sled. That's what you're destined to do."

Blix started to cry. "I don't like my destiny."

"Mama," Axel interrupted, "may I say something?"

Juno nodded. She nudged Blix lovingly with her nose.

"I think Blix should be allowed to be whatever he wants to be," Axel said. "Don't you always say that you want us to end up where we will be the happiest?"

"But, Blix, I've taught you to work the sled," Juno said.

"You also said that one day we'd grow up and leave the barn. You said we'd be sent to other farms and castles to do royal work for new families. That's what you said."

"Ah," Juno said softly. "Yes, I did say all of that."

"So, Blix wants to leave now . . . with Rex," Axel finished. "I think he should be able to go."

Juno glanced over at me and Rex. She sat there perfectly at attention, still and silent, but not angry. She was thinking.

"I don't know, Blix," Juno said. "This is most unusual. We are your family. The Winter Palace is your home."

"There's plenty of room at McDougal Palace for Blix!" Rex cried. "I just know that Annie and James will welcome a new pup!"

Juno didn't know what to say. Neither did I.

Chapter 11

"SUNNY! REX!"

Out of nowhere, I heard voices. The princess and prince were approaching the barn.

"Annie! *Rowf!*" I barked.

I ran over toward the barn door and nearly tripped over a funny comb and brush. They must have been left behind by the horse groomers.

My dull claws scratched at the barn door as if that would make it open faster. Rex came right up next to me and scratched at the door, too. Finally, the latch clicked and Annie and James burst inside.

"SUNNY! I missed you!" Annie cried, reaching for me. She looked me over, but thought better about picking me up in her arms. She had on a nubby white sweater; I would have turned it to a muddy mess!

"Looking good, Rex," James cracked. He crouched next to his messy puppy, but Rex, of course, jumped right up and left a muddy splatter on James's coat.

Rex and I each let out a wild bark. I loved our adventure in the barn, but I think I was ready to head back to McDougal Palace, to my doggy bed and all the comforts of home.

There was just the question of a certain husky dog.

What was Blix going to do now? He'd finally admitted to his mama that he did not want to be a worker dog. It had been very hard for him to do that.

Juno stretched down and lay on her belly. She was still thinking hard about what Blix had said, I could tell.

Then Annie noticed her. She let out a little scream. "Juno!?"

Of course, they knew each other. I had not really thought much about that fact until now. Juno was older and wiser than anyone in this barn.

Long before Annie came into the world,

Queen Katherine had brought Juno to McDougal Palace. She had lived and worked there for a few years, while my mama traveled around the world. Then, when she had her pups, she had been moved to the Winter Palace with Edgar, the butler, and Fitzsimmons, the cat.

The staff at McDougal Palace had been too busy awaiting the arrival of Katherine's second baby, James, to care for a husky. And after James was born, the king and queen had decided not to bring the huskies back to the palace. The dogs stayed on at Glimmer Mountain.

But Annie had had some time alone with Juno, and she had played with her from the very beginning. Now that they recognized each other, Annie embraced the mother husky as if she loved her as much as she loved me!

But I didn't mind at all.

"Oh, I've missed you, Juno!" Annie said, scratching the top of Juno's gray-and-black-speckled head. Juno's ears stood up, but her back swayed.

That dog loved being loved. That was probably what made her such a good mother to all of her husky puppies.

"Have Sunny and Rex been good pups?" Annie asked Juno.

She wagged her tail in answer.

"That was some ruckus in the palace!" Annie went on.

Juno licked her three pups and then quietly barked to Axel, Chase, and Blix, "I'll bet I know *exactly* who was responsible for all the crazy things that went on."

Axel answered, "We cleaned up our messes, Mama! We're worker dogs."

"Well, *some* of us are," Blix said quietly.

Annie noticed Blix's unhappy whimper. She bent over and hoisted Blix straight up into the air, shaking him gently back and forth.

"What's the matter, puppy? What happened? Why so blue? Cat got your tongue?"

From behind the barn door, Fitzsimmons appeared.

What was *he* doing here?

"Cat got your tongue is such a *horrible* expression," Fitz complained. "This girl and her brother know nothing about how to appreciate a palace cat."

He purred and arched his back against a post.

"Have you enjoyed your little day in the barn?" he asked Rex.

Rex was bounding about as if without a care in the world. But I cared. I was mad at this cat!

As Rex raced by, a cloud of barn dirt flew into Fitz's face. "How could you possibly have survived in all this filth?" he coughed. He wiped mud from his own face and licked his paw.

"We can survive anything!" I cried proudly. "Unlike *you*!" I flung some straw at Fitz's face. "Can you help steer a sled? No. What can you do besides meow and eat cat treats?"

Fitz made a face. "How dare you speak to me like that!" he cried.

"What I learned in the barn today," I said to Fitz, "is that palace puppies are as tough and smart as any pup. As any animal at all. And what makes us strong is kindness and love."

"What does that mean?" Fitz asked.

"Who do you love and who loves you?" I asked him.

Fitzsimmons sat silent for a moment. His tail flicked back and forth, as usual, but for once, he didn't have anything to say. His eyes glazed over.

"Don't listen to Sunny," Juno said, coming over to the cat. "Everyone at the Winter Palace loves you. *I* love you."

Fitz screeched. "Get away from me—you . . . dog! Back! Back!" He coughed again. His whole body heaved forward as he spit up another fur ball.

Juno looked hurt, but Fitzsimmons didn't say anything else. He just dashed away.

But dashing wasn't the best idea. The slippery hay on the wet floor of the barn sent him tumbling head over hind legs into a pitchfork balanced against the wall.

It came down hard on Fitz's head with a loud thunk.

We all took a deep breath.

Fitz looked a little woozy.

Everyone in the barn, including pups and ponies and the princess and prince, watched Fitz get up. He began to wander through the barn door and back out into the snow. Where was he headed? That cat was walking funny!

"I'm worried," Juno said to the other puppies. "That pitchfork must have hurt."

We watched to make sure Fitz was all right.

Of course, he wasn't.

He fell whiskers-first into a small pile of snow. When he stood up, he tripped over his own ice-covered paws!

"Oh!" Annie cried. I think we all wanted to rush out there and help him. But before any of us could make a move, Fitz stood up straight, shook himself, and turned back to face us.

"What are you looking at?" he cried.

We all stood there, with our jaws hanging open. I was hardly able to believe what I saw. That cat was covered from head to paws in spiky icicles!

"The Ice Beast lives!" Rex yelped.

I laughed out loud, even though I didn't mean to. When the other puppies laughed, too, I felt a little sorry for Fitz.

Edgar came running across the cobblestones to grab his frozen cat.

"Oh, you poor kitty," Edgar said. "Come back into the palace where it's warm and safe. Come back with me."

"Okay, pups! Now it's our turn to go back home!" Annie said, scooping me up into her arms. "Let's go, Rex."

James grabbed Rex, but that beagle would not budge.

Blix let out a sad little howl.

"What's the matter with you?" James asked.

Annie scratched her head. "Hold on, James. I think Rex is trying to tell us something."

Juno went over to Blix and nuzzled the top of her baby pup's head. Blix turned to give Juno a great big kiss.

Then Juno did something else. She nudged Blix—toward Annie and James.

Annie and James looked confused.

But then Rex and I nudged Blix toward them, too.

"James," Annie said to her brother, "I think we're supposed to take Blix home with us."

"That's weird," James said. "Can we?"

"We can ask Mother and Father, can't we?" Annie cried. "We could have a new palace puppy! That's so exciting!"

Rex's face brightened. "So we're really going to be roomies?" he asked Blix.

Blix said, "Mama says to give it a try. I can always come back to the barn if I get homesick."

I let out an enormous cheer. We were about to welcome a brand-new palace puppy! I could hardly believe it.

We said all of our good-byes to the remaining huskies. Juno gave Rex, Blix, and me lots of kisses. Annie and James gave Axel and Chase some kisses, too. Annie held Juno close. "I'll take special care of your Blix. I promise!" she said to the mama husky.

Before leaving, Annie and James made sure that we three pups had head-to-toe bubble baths. It sure was nice to have my normal furry coat back again. I was getting sick of all that mud. Blix loved the bath even more than I did. That husky was *definitely* meant to be a palace puppy. We had a long journey back down the mountain to our home, sweet home, McDougal Palace.

The trip home went surprisingly fast. Maybe it was the new company! I noticed that Rex was way less annoying when he had a playmate to keep him busy. He didn't rely on me as much as he had before.

Or maybe it was just Nanny Fran and Nanny Sarah. They kept us all entertained, with games of Who Has the Bone? and plenty of snacks.

When we finally arrived back at McDougal Palace, we were very tired. The staff had lit candles in the front entrance, but the rest of the rooms were dark, except for an occasional ray of moonlight through a window.

"Welcome home!" we barked to Blix as we walked in.

"This place is gigantic!" Blix said.

"Plenty of room to play!" Rex said.

I think Annie knew I was feeling a little bit out of sorts after our journey and the showdown with the snow monster—a.k.a. Fitzsimmons. While Rex and Blix played with a few toys, Annie kissed my snout.

"I love having a new member of the royal family, Sunny. But you're my special puppy, for always," Annie said to me. "Don't forget that."

I licked her face.

Annie went on, "It will be fun to have a new pup at the palace, won't it? You have so much to share with Blix! He's used to being in the barn. Whatever is he going to think of the bowling alley? Or the movie-screening room? Or any of the other special parts of the palace?"

I knew what he'd think of all that. *Awesome.*

At that moment, Blix bounded over toward me and Annie. He tried to jump up, even though Annie's arms were already full—with me.

I realized that I would have to get used to sharing my princess. He needed Annie's attention, too.

But I was wrong. Blix wanted *my* attention!

"Rooooowf!" Blix barked at me. "Come and play! Come and play!"

I hopped out of Annie's arms and chased Blix through the hallway, now brightly lit up on either side. We played a game of palace tag with Rex for a while, until a bell rang. Nanny Fran came to find us. She'd made a bed for Blix in James's room, alongside Rex's.

"Hey, Sunny," Blix whispered to me as we headed upstairs at bedtime. "Tomorrow, will you show me those cool bushes you told me about? You know, the ones shaped like dogs? Is there really a bush shaped like a husky? Like *me*?"

I smiled. "There really is."

Once we went upstairs, we got brushed and fluffed by Nanny Fran. Then we were sprinkled with powder—just a little, so we smelled extra nice.

In the drawing room between Annie's and James's bedrooms, there was a roaring fire burning. Seated in front of the fire were Annie and James,

both in their pajamas. While we'd been getting pampered, they'd been getting ready for bed, too. Queen Katherine and King Jon had stayed at the Winter Palace for one more night, so the princess and prince were on their own, with just Nanny Sarah and Nanny Fran.

And the puppies, of course!

"Wow, you smell good," Annie said to me as she patted my tail. "You're not the same dog I found in the barn a few hours ago!"

"Arf!" I said happily, and crawled into her lap.

Nanny Fran set some enormous pillows out on the floor a short distance from the fire. Rex and Blix playfully tossed themselves at the pillows and raced around two large leather chairs. They were still acting frisky. I couldn't believe it. I was dog-tired.

My eyes felt heavy, and soon I was fast asleep, dreaming. In my dream, *I* was the king of the castle, and I was trying my best to rule the kingdom of Glimmer Rock. Fitz was there, too, complaining about something, but I sent him away without any supper. And then I made Rex and Blix my honorary knights. I love sweet dreams like that.